Zep's Surprise

A delightful story that will melt any dog-lover's heart! *Zep's Surprise* is a heartwarming tale of a tiny, forgotten puppy that finds his way into a loving home and discovers the ultimate surprise. This story's thoughtful ending is meaningful for both parents and children alike!

Anna Benskin
Kindergarten Teacher

Zep's Surprise is a charming story of a pup, who is "different," finding love and acceptance. It will inspire many children who feel the same way Zep does and will encourage those children to find hope and confidence. I highly recommend it.

Janet Riehecky
Award-winning author of *Reptiles*

In the heart of every child is a lurking, unspoken fear that they are not loved. This engaging and powerful story will delight children and convey to them the most important message they could ever hear. That message is that God loves them unconditionally. I highly recommend this book!

Rob Currie, Ph.D.
Professor of Psychology, Judson University
Author of *Hunger Winter*

Zep's Surprise is a precious children's book that draws kids and adults alike into the world of a less-than-perfect puppy who learns what it means to be loved and treasured. Written through the eyes of Zep, the runt of a dachshund litter, the story begins as Zep is adopted, meets his new mommy and daddy, and is given a new name and a new home. He learns that he always is loved by his family and by God, no matter what scary things happen to him! This sweet story will help children understand what it means to be treasured by God and will remind them over and over how much God truly loves them!

Carol Thompson
Retired executive of *Christianity Today*

"Inspirational," said my young grandson, gleefully. Reading together about Zep the dachshund will help children find healthy acceptance of themselves and others through God's special design.

Ronald Bennett
Professional Counselor

When I read this book for the first time, it brought tears to my eyes. So many people (and dogs!) in the world long to know unconditional love. Through Zep's story, we read how God loves each of us with all our unique attributes. I found it an encouraging reminder that we can all find a place to call home.

Kristy Engel, MSN, RN, CPNP-PC
Faith Community Nurse,
Global Consultant for Health, International Ministries,
ABC-USA

As a fellow dachshund enthusiast, of course I loved *Zep's Surprise*! It's a sweet story of a little puppy who wasn't like all the others and felt he didn't measure up. Then he was chosen by a family and greatly loved, even though he wasn't perfect. I identified with the story because we adopted a baby girl years ago who grew up to be different; not like all the others. Yet we loved her; and more importantly, God loved her, and she grew up to feel very loved and wanted, just like Zep. This is a great story for anyone who has someone "not like all the others" in their lives or for those who have "perfect" families who need to be reminded how much God loves us—all of us.

Maralee Parker
Author of *Unexpected: A Memoir of Endurance and Triumph in Raising a Challenging Child*

Zep's Surprise is a very sweet, beautifully written, and wonderfully illustrated story about God's love for a very special puppy. It will truly touch your heart. It teaches us about God's love and how He loves and treasures each one of us. It shows us how He made each one of us very remarkable and special. This is a wonderful book to share with your children and grandchildren. I would definitely use this book in my classroom. I would say it's a must-read for all kindergarten and lower elementary teachers to read to their students. I promise it will warm your heart!

Sandee Ashby
Retired teacher
Valor Christian Academy, Redondo Beach, California

Zep's Surprise

Randy Gauger

Illustrated by Sophia Duguid

You are treasured by God!

Randy Gauger

Psalm 106:1

Ambassador International
Greenville, South Carolina & Belfast, Northern Ireland

www.ambassador-international.com

Zep's Surprise

©2024 Randy Gauger
All rights reserved.

This book or any portion thereof may not be reproduced or used in any manner whatsoever without the express written permission of the author and publisher, except for the use of brief quotations in a book review.

ISBN: 978-1-64960-405-7, hardcover

ISBN: 978-1-64960-406-4, paperback

eISBN: 978-1-64960-454-5

Edited by Shannon Milligan

Illustrated by Sophia Duguid

Cover and Interior Layout by Karen Slayne

Digital Edition by Anna Riebe Raats

AMBASSADOR INTERNATIONAL
Emerald House
411 University Ridge, Suite B14
Greenville, SC. 29601
www.ambassador-international.com

AMBASSADOR INTERNATIONAL BOOKS
The Mount
2 Woodstock Link
Belfast, BT6 8DD, Northern Ireland, UK
www.ambassadormedia.co.uk

The colophon is a trademark of Ambassador, a Christian publishing company.

ACKNOWLEDGMENTS

I am grateful to my wife, Mary, for her encouragement and support in writing *Zep's Surprise*. She lived this story with me. She gracefully endured my hours at the computer and made suggestions along the way as the story came to life. Mary advocated for Ambassador International as the ideal publisher if they would partner with me. Thank you, Mary, and thank you, Ambassador.

Several published writers met regularly at Judson University to discuss their writing projects. By God's grace, I was included in that group. Their insightful coaching to help me shape this story was invaluable. Thank you, Judson writing friends.

To work with our granddaughter, Sophia Duguid, who illustrated *Zep's Surprise*, has been a joy. Her talent, now embedded in this story, will bring to mind our many conversations about the illustrations she created. Thank you, Sophia, for sharing the amazing gifts God has given you.

Sophia's father, Stirling Duguid, also provided priceless help. His natural artistic ability and his expertise in working with animated features in the movie industry have been an immeasurable resource in the design and flow of *Zep's Surprise*. Thank you, Stirling.

I believe the Holy Spirit prompted me to write this story. My prayer is that He who began this work (Phil. 1:6) will cause it to flourish in all who read and hear this story. To God be the glory!

Zep's Surprise

is lovingly dedicated to our grandchildren: Caleb Loeppky (and wife, Cassidy), Anna Benskin (and husband, Branden), Emma Camacho (and husband, Francisco), Nailah Loeppky, Miyah Loeppky, Sophia Duguid (illustrator), Caden Duguid, Chloe Duguid; and our great-grandchildren, Nora Loeppky, Jaxon Loeppky, and Asher Loeppky.

The hard floor in my fenced run hurt my feet. Still, Zeke, Charlie, Mo, Penny, and I chased around and nipped and barked in each other's faces.

They were all bigger dachshunds.

Why am I so small?
I'm six months old.

The lady who cared for us shouted to me, "You! Come."

Why don't I have a name?
When people came to our yard,
they called me Runt,
but I wanted a real name.

Every day, my lady brought our food.
I licked my chops and tried to
wiggle around my brothers and sister,
but they pushed harder.

Often, I didn't get enough food.

When my brothers and sister
were six months old,
they started going to dog shows.

Take me,

I yearned and jumped.

But my lady looked at me and said,
"Your tail is twisted.
You'll never get to go to dog shows."

When I was formed inside my mother,
I didn't grow like other dogs.
My tail was crooked.
My father was a champion,
but I was not.

One day, my lady gave me a bath and trimmed my nails. Baths are awful, but when she walked me to the car, my tail wagged rapidly—a car ride!

Am I going to a dog show?

We stopped at a restaurant parking lot. She took me out of the car and set me on the ground. Two people I'd never seen stared at me.

I wondered what they smelled like,
so I went slowly to them, putting my head
down and turning it to one side and then
another, again and again. As I got close,
they giggled and stroked my back.

"Hello, little guy," they said, scratching my ears.
"Someone told us, 'If a dog walks to you,
he likes you,'" they told my lady.

Don't stop touching me and talking to me.

Suddenly, they stepped away. My ears dropped.

Are you leaving? Don't go,

I thought, as I whined and jumped toward them.

"We'd like to take him home with us," they offered as they walked back to my lady.

What does that mean?

As the strangers returned, my tail wagged uncontrollably. They picked me up and put me in the backseat of their car.

They want me?
Do they know my tail is twisted?

My lady walked to their car and explained that she had not given me a name because she wanted my forever family to choose my name.

That's why I don't have a name!

"He barks a lot," she blurted.

Don't tell them that!

I fretted. But again, they said they wanted me.

As we rode along, I got sleepy but couldn't close my eyes. I looked around the car, out the window and at the people taking me.

I listened as they talked. "He'll need food, a bed, doctor's care, and toys; he'll want to go on walks."

Toys? Walks?

My tail twitched wildly. They talked about how much they could enjoy me. Yet I shook.

Where am I going?

"What's the matter?" they asked. "It's okay."
I cowered back in the seat.

"What should we name him?" they asked each other as we finally stopped.

I put my front paws on the door to look out the window.

Is this where they live?
Will this be my home?

My tail swayed back and forth.

They carried me into their house.

Wow, this floor is so soft on my feet!
What's that over there? It looks soft, too.
Maybe I can sleep there.

I explored every room.

They said they wanted a perfect name for me. They went to look up dog names in a place where they had many books. After looking for a while, they brought those books home. Later, they opened them again and kept searching for a name.

"How about this one?" they asked each other. Again and again, they said, "No, not that one."

Suddenly, the woman smiled and pointed to a three-letter name: Zep. They said it was short for a man in the Bible who spoke for God; his name was Zephaniah.

**"Zep? Zep!"
They're talking to me!**

My tail shook.
My whole body danced.
I ran around the room.
I have a name! I am Zep!

"Zephaniah means
'God has treasured' or
'God protects,'" they discussed quietly.
"We protect what we treasure,
and we treasure what we love."

My ears perked up.

God treasures me? Smallest of my family?
With a crooked tail?
My head tilted curiously.

"Everything God makes is special," they continued.
So, God is not like the judges at dog shows.

I have a new mommy and daddy, a new family!

I sat on my back legs and gazed at them
as my eyes blinked repeatedly.

Then I lay down, rested my chin and front paws
on the soft rug, and dozed. I knew I was finally home.

One day, I sensed danger.
I must safeguard my family.
So, I barked.

Mommy and Daddy's eyes opened wide.
I'd never barked since they brought me home.
**But it's my duty.
I have to protect my family!**

"She told us he barks a lot," they agreed.

One day, Mommy put a little ball next to my food bowl.
What's this?
I puzzled.

I tapped it with my nose, and it rolled across the floor as I ate. She laughed, so I did it again. If the ball rolled too far, I ran to get it, put it by my bowl again, tapped it, and watched it move across the floor again. She chuckled, patted me on the head, and said, "Zep, you're funny!"

Is this what it's like to be treasured?

They got me a small, rubber dumbbell to play with outdoors. They threw it across the yard, and I dashed to find it, then brought it back and dropped it by the deck door. With my back legs hunched up and front legs stretched in front of me, I focused on the dumbbell and hoped they would throw it again. If they didn't see me, I tapped on the glass door with my paw. Daddy came and threw it again, and I ran to bring it back. I never knew being loved could be so much fun.

One evening, I rested on Mommy as she lay on the couch. Daddy went to the refrigerator. Thinking he was getting food, I sat up and turned quickly to look, but I hurt my long back very badly. Soon, I could not stand, walk, or move my back legs. I breathed heavily and cried.

Will Mommy and Daddy love me if I can't walk?

I worried.

Daddy took me to a doctor, who said I had seriously injured my back and needed an operation, or I might never walk again.

Daddy became very quiet. They took me to an animal hospital and had to leave me there. My back ached.

What will happen to me?

I don't know anyone here.

I'm afraid.

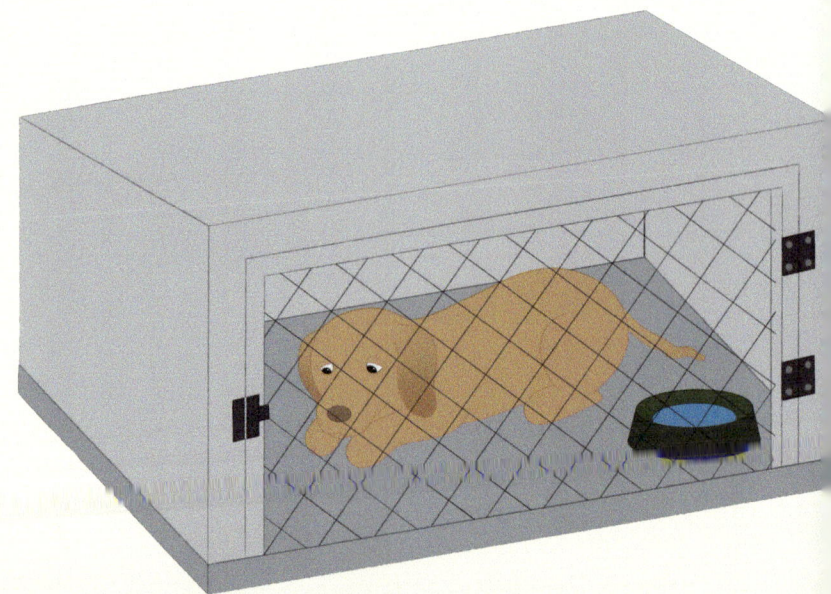

Doctors operated on my back. When Daddy and Mommy came back to see me, I whimpered happily but still could not move my back legs.

Do they still believe God treasures me? Am I still special?

When I got home, Mommy and Daddy worked with me daily. Daddy laid me on my back and worked my legs like bicycle pedals trying to get them to move on their own. Mommy walked me in a tub of water, but I could move only my front legs; my back legs floated behind me.

They continued working with me for weeks. Doctors checked my progress and one day saw tiny movement in my legs. I was healing!

After many exercises, I could walk again and eventually run. But sometimes, it was like a rabbit hopping.

Will my family love me if I don't walk like other dogs?

But if I walked slower, they walked slower. They stopped, rubbed my back, and said, "It's okay, Zep. We love you just the way you are."

As I grew older, a swelling the size of a golf ball grew on my chest. The doctor didn't remove it because it wasn't harmful and would grow back. My family looked sad when people laughed at it or said it was ugly.

Now, when Mommy or Daddy pet me or hold me, I close my eyes and never move. I love being loved.

Mommy and Daddy's children and grandchildren carry me like a baby, hug me, play with me, and take me on walks. I go on many car rides, and I love to play with my dog cousins. I have a wonderful life.

God treasures me, and so does my family. They say I'm a gift from God. What a wondrous surprise!

God treasures you, too. No matter who you are, what's happened to you, or what you look like, you are treasured by God. I know that. My name is Zep—one of God's treasures. You are, too, because everything God makes is special.

> "This is what love is:
> it is not that we have loved God,
> but that he loved us …"
>
> 1 John 4:10a, GNB

ABOUT THE AUTHOR

Randy Gauger is a retired pastor who lives in
Sycamore, Illinois, with his wife, Mary, and their dog, Moses.

You may contact Randy at
www.facebook.com/randy.gauger
or on his blog, Randy's Ruminating, at www.randygauger.com

ABOUT THE ILLUSTRATOR

Sophia Duguid lives in North Vancouver, B.C.,
with her family and their dog, Maisie.
Sophia is the granddaughter of Randy and Mary.

The Real Zep

Ambassador International's mission is to magnify the Lord Jesus Christ and promote His Gospel through the written word.

For more information about
AMBASSADOR INTERNATIONAL
please visit:

www.ambassador-international.com
www.facebook.com/AmbassadorIntl
@AmbassadorIntl

Thank you for reading this book.
Please consider leaving us a review on your social media, favorite retailer's website, Goodreads, Bookbub, or our website.

Also Available from Ambassador International

Guess How Much God Loves You is the story of seven-year-old Lucy Lu, a colorful, creatively curious first-grader, who is starting to have serious questions about God. How old is He? Does He sleep? What does He do all day? And the biggest one of all—does God love me? After one particularly hard day of being bullied by her classmates at school, Lucy feels like she doesn't matter. She sits with Papa Joe, who has promised to answer her questions about God, launching them onto a journey to discover God's never-changing, never-failing, never-ending love. What follows is a wild adventure through the Bible, where Lucy and her papa find themselves in the middle of each page of the exciting story of God's love and faithfulness for all people throughout all of history.

Sky, a boisterous young pup, and her family are enjoying a day at the lake when they discover a sore in Sky's mouth. A trip to the veterinarian's office soon reveals Sky has cancer. Not giving up hope, Sky's family and friends turn to prayer for her healing.

Although a sensitive topic for children, *Miraculous Sky* is a resource for families going through a similar situation. This uplifting children's book reminds us that we can turn to God for comfort and guidance during difficult times. It also teaches children how to trust God with their needs.